THE MAGIC SKATEBOARD

Enid Richemont

Illustrations by Jan Ormerod

WALKER BOOKS

AND SUBSIDIARIES

LONDON • BOSTON • SYDNEY

For Danny

First published 1991 by Walker Books Ltd
87 Vauxhall Walk, London SE11 5HJ

This edition published 1999

Text © 1991 Enid Richemont
Illustrations © 1991 Jan Ormerod

2 4 6 8 10 9 7 5 3 1

Printed in England by Clays Ltd, St Ives plc

British Library Cataloguing in Publication Data
A catalogue record for this book
is available from the British Library.

ISBN 0-7445-5277-X

CONTENTS

Chapter One

It was exactly five days before Christmas.

It was a day when you could do anything.

They'd brought in biscuits and crisps and popped open cans of fizzy drinks.

They'd painted their faces and put on a pantomime.

They'd yelled, "See you next year!" to Mr O'Sullivan.

At four o'clock it was already dusk. The first star glimmered through the football netting, and the light from the street lamps brushed silver over leaves as brittle as brandy-snaps.

The last teacher to leave called out, "Watch it, you lot! You'll be locked in!"

Danny and his gang, puffing like dragons, squeaked open the school gate and stood huddled on the pavement.

Usually they would have hung around until five or even later, for they all lived close by. But it was cold. Too cold for snow even, people were saying, and too chilly to fool about in the street, when every lit window was making them think of warmth and food and television.

So they broke up.

"See ya..."

"Bye..."

Danny had lost his gloves, and his fingers ached with the cold. He put down his skateboard and scraped slowly along the frost-powdered pavement, thinking of supper and Christmas, and Christmas and supper.

He didn't hear the lady coming. He didn't see her until his face hit something soft and squidgy, and his nose was tickled by a feathery thing that smelt of cinnamon and mothballs.

"Sorry," he said. It was always happening, he thought, and it wasn't fair. *He* had to balance. All they had to do was walk.

He sneezed.

"Bless you."

Danny looked up at her.

Up and up...

And up.

For she was the tallest woman Danny had ever seen, and certainly the strangest. Her ragged velvet coat was the colour of ripe damsons, and an inch or two of tattered silk skirt drooped over boots as glossy as a beetle's back. Her scarf of black ostrich feathers brushed the ground, and a black straw hat trimmed with sugar violets was tied under her chin with black netting. Her hair – the little he could see of it – was white, and

her face as wrinkled as a prune, but her eyes were bright and wickedly alert.

Danny stared at her. He just couldn't help it.

"That is an interesting toy you have," she said at last. "A … skateboard, I believe it is called."

Her voice was clear and strong, but she said her words a little too carefully, as if she had just learned them from a book.

Silly old sausage, thought Danny; a skateboard isn't a toy.

He nodded.

"That's right."

"May I look at it?"

No, you can't, he thought crossly, handing it over.

He saw her long, black-gloved fingers moving over the board, stroking its surface, touching its curved edges, as if she had never seen anything quite like it.

Danny watched her in amazement. Lots of people had skateboards. Where had she come from?

She was probably potty.

She was probably nuts.

And old. Even older than his gran...

She started playing with the rollers. They seemed to fascinate her. With a flick of her fingers, she set them spinning. The spinning seemed to please her, and she did it again. And again. And again.

Just like my kid brother, thought Danny scornfully. Just like some itsy-witsy baby.

Then she smiled – the small, satisfied smile people give when they've just finished making something.

"Thank you." She handed it back to him.

Danny tucked it under his arm. He wriggled uncomfortably, feeling her watching him, her eyes twinkling, her face crinkling, as if they were sharing some special secret.

"Are you," she said, "very skilful at this ... skateboarding?"

Danny shrugged.

He was working at it, wasn't he?

Anyway, what did she know?

"Watch this," he said, crossing his fingers.

He put down the board and skated a short distance along the street. Concentrating hard, he performed a shaky kick-turn, flapping his arms about to balance. Then he came right back at her, only swerving aside at the last minute.

Scared you! Scared you! he thought gleefully, hoping she'd squeal and jump, like his sister always did.

But she just went on standing there. Looking at him.

Danny picked up his board.

He was cold.

He was hungry.

And anyway, his mum didn't like him talking to strangers.

Chapter Two

"Wait!"

The woman's voice was unexpectedly bossy.

Danny hesitated.

She smiled.

"May I try?" she asked politely.

He blinked. She had to be joking.

But she slid the skateboard from under his arm and set it down on the ground.

Danny watched, speechless.

Well, what was there to say?

Weird, he thought. A real nutcase.

She kicked off. He held his breath.

"You'll fall," he shouted, but somehow he knew that her balance would be perfect.

And it was.

She skated to the end of the street, a ridiculous figure, her long skirts flapping in the breeze, and the feather scarf curling around her like a flying caterpillar. She turned and came back.

"I shall try some turns now," she said.

"Oh, no!" protested Danny. "I mean, you need to be good to do turns. I mean, you need

to practise. And you ought to have knee
pads..."

The woman ignored him.

Delicately she placed one black boot
on the skateboard.

"Is this how you start?"

She pushed off sideways.
She closed her eyes and
began to spin. Faster
and faster. The board
was moving so quickly
now that Danny
could no longer
make out
its shape.

The coat and the ragged skirt whirled into a plum-coloured spinning top. Her face spun like white candy-floss, but her eyes kept watching him – her eyes like shiny black grapes, dark and wicked, teasing him.

She slowed down and stopped.

"I did not fall," she said smugly.

Danny drew a breath. "Can I have it back now?" he asked in a small voice.

"Be patient..."

She began to fool round with the skateboard, rocking it from side to side across the pavement.

Danny was worried. It *had* been his birthday present.

"OK, so you're good..." he muttered.

She began to bounce it against a front garden wall.

"Oh stop it!" he shouted.

She began to slide up the garden wall. Up and up. She slid over the neat privet hedge – he could hear the rollers scraping over frozen leaves.

For a second she disappeared. Then he saw her. She was skateboarding up the front of the house, carefully avoiding the windows. In one of those windows, a girl, her back to the street, was looping a paper streamer round the bars of her bunk bed. Danny gawped in disbelief. That girl had seen nothing; knew nothing...

"Danny!"

He looked up, and there was the woman, sitting astride the roof, laughing, waving. In one hand she held his skateboard.

"Catch!" she shouted.

"Oh no!" yelled Danny, but his hands shot out and the skateboard fell into them as gently as a beachball.

"It's yours," she said.

"I know," said Danny.

"But it is also mine..."

Danny's watch began to bleep. Irritated, he switched it off. Then he noticed the time. Not yet five. It shouldn't have done that...

High above his head, the woman was chuckling.

"My time," she said. "We share it. Until your watch speaks again, do with it whatever you wish. And a Merry Christmas to you!"

She took a backwards somersault into the air. For one moment she hung, suspended

between roof-top and sky. Then, stretching out an arm like a swimmer she began to glide in a great curve, over the street, over the school at the end of the street, and away.

Danny watched, open-mouthed, running, moving to follow the path of her flight. He watched until the flapping skirts and the pale face became nothing but a violet rag blown by the wind. He watched until they turned into a thin line drawn with a purple crayon, and he watched that line until it winked out of sight somewhere over the park. Even then he went on looking, half expecting her to reappear, listening for her mocking laughter.

After a while, his neck began to ache. He shook himself and looked around.

It was the same old street. Nothing had changed. There were the frozen plane trees with their dappled trunks. There was the street lamp someone had smashed. There were the rude words sprayed on the wall, and there, at the end of the street, rose the dark, familiar shape of his school. The same old cars were parked along the road – the red Mini and the dirty van with "WASH ME" finger-painted in dust.

Pop music suddenly blared from an open door. A cat howled.

Danny shivered.

She'd fooled him, he thought. It had all been a trick.

And anyway, he was hungry.

Chapter Three

Danny looked at his skateboard.

It was the same skateboard. A good one, but ordinary. Nothing special about it, apart from the fact that months ago, his dad had given it to him for his birthday.

He thought again about those stunts the old lady had pulled off. They had to be a trick. You just couldn't do things like that on a skateboard. Even if you were good. Even if you were a champ. Nobody could.

He wondered if she'd fiddled with it in some way, damaged it, messed it about. Worried, he put it down on the pavement. He stepped on to it, trying it out, rocking it gently from side to side. She had skateboarded over the hedge – now *that* was impossible. And up the front of the house.

How did it feel, he wondered, to skateboard up the front of a house?

At once, he knew. Up and over the hedge he went.

He should have fallen off.

He did not.

He should have been terrified.
He was not.
Below him,
the gardens
and the street
moved rapidly
away as Danny
carefully avoided
the windows.
And up the
side of the
roof he went
until he stood
at the
very top.

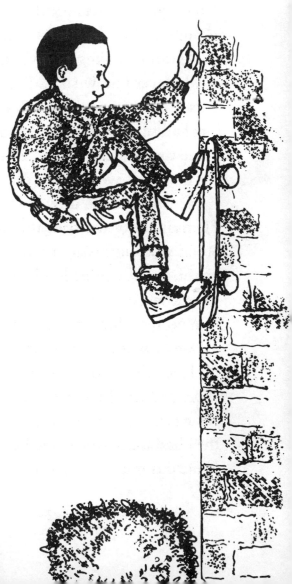

He wasn't scared. He knew he wouldn't fall. He didn't know how he knew. He just knew.

He was a bird. He was a Golden Eagle. He was Superman. He could do anything on that skateboard. Anything at all...

My time, she'd said. We share it... Do with it whatever you wish...

Now he understood. Whatever you wish, she had said. Whatever you wish...

He took a deep breath and thought of the pavement. It worked! In one smooth movement he was down. This was fantastic! He thought of the roof-top and once again he stood with his head in the sky. Down he went again, laughing out loud. Up and down. Up and down.

Who was the greatest?

Danny was the greatest!

He longed to show someone. He wanted to shock passers-by but there were no passers-by. He wanted to show off to his friends but they had long since gone home. He thought about his mum, who always said she was

unshockable. He thought about his older
sister who teased him, and his little brother
who pestered him.

And instantly he was in his own front
garden. A cat sprang into the air, hissed,
and vanished through a hole in the hedge.
He giggled. Wait till his mum saw him
skating up the roof...

He was going to ring the bell when he
paused. Until your watch speaks again, she'd
said; it might do that right now. He looked
down at it. The numbers hadn't
changed. So how much
time *did* he have?
And how much
of it might he
waste, trying
to persuade
his mum to come
out and watch?
She'd probably
witter on about
lateness, and make him

put the skateboard away and come in and
eat his supper.

So how long? Ten minutes? Fifteen minutes?

Thoughtfully, he skated up
the front of his house. Susie
was looking at her face
in the mirror. She was
always looking at her
face in the mirror.

For a while
he balanced on
the roof-top, breathing
the icy air and looking at
the stars – they seemed much
closer up there. He leapt on to a
chimney-pot, perching there like a
giant crow. Then, punctuating roofs with
chimney-pots and chimney-pots with roofs,
he skated joyfully down the street.

He thought of his school, and in an instant
he was on the roof, looking down into the
empty playground. It worked! It worked!

Danny jumped into the air.

"I am the Champion!" he shouted, beating his chest.

There was no one to hear.

"I can do anything!"

There was no one there to argue. It was too cold. Even Danny was cold. Especially his fingers.

He wondered if he could use his magic to find his gloves. He filled his mind with a picture of them. Red, woolly and warm. Nice gloves. His gran had made them for him. He wished himself to be wherever they were.

The skateboard began to move. Down the front of the building it slid and across the playground. Outside the infants' annexe it stopped. Now that was wrong – Danny was no infant. He wondered if the magic was already beginning to fade. He listened for the bleeps, but his watch was silent.

He tried again, thinking about his lost gloves, even remembering the hole in the thumb.

"Take me," he said, "to my gloves!" It sounded very silly.

And nothing happened at all.

Disappointed, he looked reproachfully down at the skateboard and there, on the ground, lay a single familiar red glove. Just one.

Astonished, he bent down and picked it up. It was frozen – stiff as the hand of a puppet. He was thinking, not much use to me, when there was a swoosh and a crackle and a snap, and Danny found himself in complete darkness.

Chapter Four

Danny should have been frightened.

He was not.

He was curious, though. The place he was in smelt familiar but he couldn't think why.

He put out his hands like a blind man and his fingers closed around a soft woolly object with an odd metal spine. He pulled at the woolly thing. It came off in his hand. It was his glove. His other glove.

Danny grinned.

Of course.

He knew where he was.

He felt his way along a row of curved metal spines. He knew what they were.

Just past the place where they ended, he knew there would be a door. He found it. He opened it. Behind the door he knew there would be a light switch. He flipped it on. From the rows of pegs in the school cloakroom, a couple of forgotten plimsoll bags drooped heavily, like over-ripe pears.

Pleased with himself, Danny picked up his skateboard and walked out into the dim

corridor. He could just make out the
paintings pinned to the wall, and the
Christmas decorations. He switched on
another light. The polished wooden floor
stretched out deliciously in front of him.
Skateboarding, he knew, was strictly
forbidden inside school...

Down the corridor whizzed Danny, down
the corridor and into the hall, flipping light
switches on the way. Round
the hall he skated,
round and round
it and across
the platform
and over
the piano
and round
again.

He thought of Assembly, and giggled – if only his teachers could see him now...

He began to sing a carol, shouting out the words. He knew the words of all of them, because he was in the choir. He knew another version of this one. A rude version, which had nothing to do with Christmas... He sang that one too. He sang it at the top of his voice.

When he stopped, the hall was uncomfortably quiet. It was like that awkward silence that happens when nobody knows what to say next.

Danny didn't know what to do next.

He tried transferring himself to his classroom. How strange it looked at night. How dark and empty. He switched on the light and skated across the desk tops. He tried a dozen kick-turns on his teacher's table, and every one was perfect. A packet of chalk fell to the ground. He stopped and picked it up. The surface of the blackboard had been wiped clean.

Danny looked at it and grinned.

Then he shook out
the chalk and began to
write:

HAPPY NEW YEAR
TO EVERYBODY.

LOVE DANNY.

He had just got to the
"Y" of YEAR when he
heard a noise. The sound
of a key being turned
in a lock. Footsteps.
Somebody shouting.
It was the caretaker.
Danny froze. Now he was for it. Now
there'd be trouble. Breaking and entering –
would they ring for the police? He dropped
his chalk, picked up his skateboard and
started to run.
Then he stopped.
Who was a dumb-dumb?

Who was a twit?

He put down his skateboard and stepped on to it.

The caretaker came running along the corridor, a torch in his hand. Their eyes met.

"What the...?" he exclaimed.

"Hampstead Heath!" yelled Danny.

Chapter Five

There was a sound like a small firework
exploding, and a rush of icy air, and the
caretaker's startled eyes and his gaping mouth
disappeared into a whirling patchwork of
black woods and street lights.

Suddenly Danny found himself standing on
the top of a dark hill. Grey grass sloped into
shadows, and disappeared into dim huddles
of trees. Below him, through the frosty air, he
could see the city sprinkled across the night
like a bowlful of sequins.

Wow! he thought.

He'd been to the Heath before, but never at night. This was brilliant. He could have stayed up there for hours.

He didn't really know why he'd asked for it – it had just been the first name that had popped into his head:

Hampstead Heath,
Clean your teeth...

He could have asked for home.

He could have wished himself into his best friend's house.

He just hadn't had time to think.

Now he did.

So the skateboard could travel this far...

How much further?

The big McDonald's in Piccadilly Circus? But he had no money. A cinema, then; he could get in for free. But there wouldn't be time to see the film. London Airport; he could watch the planes. The seaside? He shivered: too cold. What about France, then, where he'd spent his summer holidays?

What about Africa?

He grinned.

Now he *was* being silly...

Her time, she'd said. Whatever that was. He looked nervously down at his watch, but he couldn't see the numbers. Her time... How much of it had he used up already?

"Too much..."

He whipped round but there was no one there.

"You're wasting it..."

He caught a whiff of cinnamon and mothballs.

"Where are you?" he called.

"You have not even started..."

He looked up, and there she
was, hanging by her boots
from the sky, her pale face
with its wicked dark
eyes and flowered
hat just a few
yards above
his head.

"Stop gaping, boy, and get on with it."

Danny gasped.

"How do you do that?" he said but she'd already gone.

Get on with it…

All right, then. He would.

He took a deep breath.

"Trafalgar Square!"

He skated into the air. The hill he had been standing on fell rapidly backwards, and the whole Heath suddenly opened like a fan below him, dark and mysterious. He moved so quickly that the stars above his head turned into a silver scrawl, and all the little cars on the streets below became threads of gold and orange and red.

He began to hear voices. People singing. Water splashing.

A fine spray spattered his cheeks. He was skating round the edge of a fountain. Round and round and round.

Nobody saw him. All the people were

looking at an enormous Christmas tree
glittering with lights.

Danny jumped down. He picked up his
skateboard and wriggled through the crowd,
but he was too small to see over people's
shoulders. He wondered if he should wish
himself closer, but there was surely no room,
even for magic.

People jostled around him in a friendly sort
of way, like people at a party. Most of them
were singing. A little kid pushed past him,
stepping on his toes, yelling for his daddy.

With nothing better to do, Danny joined in the carol, but his eyes were already sliding past the big star at the top of the tree, past the fountains and the crouching lions, to something much taller. Something much higher than the Christmas tree. Something with a stone man standing on top, whose hat pointed into the sky.

Danny wondered what sort of a view Nelson had up there...

Suddenly faces turned into tops of heads. Then heads became blobs, lions became pussy cats, and offices, theatres and government buildings went swooshing into the ground. And the wind whistled past Danny's ears as he skated up and up, to balance breathless at the top, his hand on a cold stone knee.

Only three people saw a boy skateboarding up the side of Nelson's Column.

The first was a poet who smiled, nibbled the end of his pencil, then wrote in a small blue notebook:

OLD WARRIOR
STONE WARRIOR
PUT UP YOUR SWORD
FOR A BOY ON A SKATEBOARD
IS COMING ABOARD...

The second was an old man who carried a notice on a stick. The notice said: BEWARE OF THE WRATH TO COME. When the old man saw Danny, he pointed a quivering finger.

"Behold!" he said. "Angels are already amongst us..."

But nobody listened. Nobody ever listened.

The third was a fat five-year-old girl, who tugged at her mother's sleeve.

"Look, Mum! That boy's going up Nelson's Column on a skateboard!"

"Shut up," said her mum, without turning her head. "You've been watching too much telly..."

Chapter Six

Furious pigeons flapped into the air, their familiar roosts disturbed by a great boy who had no business being there at all.

And it was cold. It was so cold that Danny almost forgot to look down.

But beside him, Nelson stared into the night, touched neither by cold nor Christmas, and around them both, the wind howled, and above them both, the stars glittered icily. Danny shivered. The world below him looked unreal. The Christmas tree he'd wanted to see was just a tinselly toy. The cars were toys, and all the little heads in the crowd were bobbing like flowers in a meadow. Nothing was real, except the wind lashing his cheeks.

A pigeon landed on Danny's head; he could feel the

scritch-scratch of its feet in his hair as it
marched about. It was heavy, too; he'd never
thought a bird could be as heavy as that.
Now he knew how it felt to be a statue.
Except that statues didn't feel. Not pigeons.
Not anything. Not even the cold...

Especially the cold.

Lucky things, thought Danny.

He began to think about warmth. Radiators.
Fires. Mugs of hot chocolate. Bowls of soup.
Sun. Summer. Beaches... He remembered the
beach where he'd played in the holidays. He
remembered the feeling of warm sand running
through his fingers, of jumping into the sea to
cool down. Summer was like a dream...

A beach like that, he thought, would be
lovely now...

He hadn't meant to make such a very clear
picture come into his head. The sand between
his toes. The shells. The blue-green water
glinting in the sun...

That was what he was thinking as he rose
into the night.

That was what he was thinking as he watched Trafalgar Square turn into a pattern of lights. A small pattern inside a big one. The big one was London.

The big one became small and vanished. Other patterns took its place. They vanished too. And all the time the stars drew silver threads across an inky sky.

The sky greyed and the threads broke. The sky became primrose and they vanished. Below him lay camouflage country in greens and browns. Below him lay a range of mountains covered in snow. More camouflage country and more mountains. Lakes like shiny coins. Rivers like curly ribbons. Seas. Oceans...

Now he saw a great bridge spanning a harbour.

The skateboard scrunched against sand.
It was hot. It was very hot.

Danny was sweating. He took off his socks
and shoes and curled his bare toes in the
sand. The sand was the colour of caramel
cream, and people lay all over it, basking in
the heat like contented seals. Near him a
man and a woman were cuddling. Nobody
noticed Danny.

He stood up and looked round. Behind him rose an olive-green lattice of trees. Through it, on a road, he could see cars twinkling. Somewhere, someone began playing a guitar.

Danny wondered where he was. He wondered where in the world it could be hot and sunny five days before Christmas. Not France, certainly. Africa, perhaps? America? How far had he travelled? How far had he come? He looked at the place where the ocean met the sky.

Which ocean?

He gave up, and watched the waves instead. He watched them growing and curling into breakers. He watched the breakers falling in fountains of white foam. People were surfing in that ocean, their boards skimming the water, light as leaves.

An orange butterfly settled on the back of his hand. He watched it lazily. Surfing, he thought. Must be a bit like skateboarding...

He looked at the skateboard lying at his feet.

He looked at his watch. It wasn't five yet.
How much time did he have?

He took off his anorak. He took off his
jeans and his pullover and his shirt. He picked
up his skateboard and ran to the edge of the
ocean. Foam creamed around his toes, and his
feet sank two hollows into the wet sand.

He put the skateboard down, and stepped
on to it.

Somebody laughed.

Somebody shouted, "You can't surf on that thing, sport!"

He could, of course.

And he did.

No problem...

For Danny rode the waves like a small sea-god, sliding up the curved green walls of water and gliding along inside them. The tops of the waves, where they broke and met the sky, were full of dancing lights. The depths were like old bottles – lustrous greens and smoky browns and amber like his mum's ear-rings. Never in his life had he seen anything so marvellous. He could have gone on doing this for ever.

Almost weeping, he forced himself to turn back to the beach. How much time had he used up now?

And how would he get home if all the magic ran out?

As he waded out of the water a boy came up to him.

"You can't surf on one of those things," he said.

"Well, I just have," said Danny.

"I know," said the boy admiringly. "What's the trick?"

Danny shrugged.

"It's easy, really," he said modestly. "Nothing to it, if you know how..."

He walked up the beach feeling rather superior.

The other boy tagged on behind.

"Show me," he was saying. "Will you? Will you show me?"

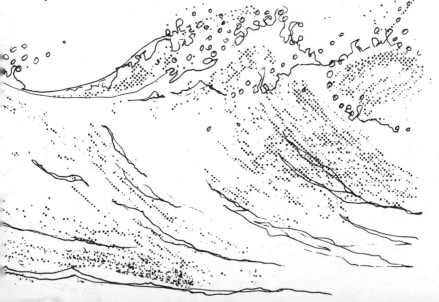

Danny struggled into his clothes, grateful that his underpants had dried so quickly in the hot sun. He was beginning to worry. How much time was left? Would she warn him?

Perhaps he should go home right now...

Then he thought of something quite ridiculous.

Really silly.

Wicked....

He grinned.

For he had a cousin. And his cousin lived in France.

He would stop off and visit him. On his way home. From wherever he was. Wish him a Merry Christmas. Give him a shock...

He thought about his cousin's house. His room...

The other boy was saying, "Why you need an anorak in the middle of December?"

But the rest of his words were lost.

Chapter Seven

The ocean fell away.

Then it was gone, swallowed by the olive and gold of the land.

Mountains.

Valleys.

He was flying backwards into dawn. The sky paled, blushed, then burned with orange fire. It yellowed, turned lime, blued, turned violet, greyed and deepened into night. Stars silvered the night sky. The moon rolled round like an ivory ball. Cities twinkled and vanished. Clouds grew, spread and blackened and lightning streaked across them. Then they shrank and disappeared. Thunder crashed, growled and faded into a thin whine. It rained; then stopped. Danny put out his tongue and caught a snowflake.

Then he was in his cousin's room, sitting on the floor.

Matthew was lying on the bed, reading a comic.

"Hi, Matt," said Danny, shaking raindrops out of his hair.

Matthew looked cross.

"You splashed me," he said.

Then he sat up very straight and his eyes grew large.

"You're in England."

"That's right," agreed Danny cheerfully. "I just popped over to wish you a Merry Christmas!"

He suddenly panicked.

"Got to pee," he yelled. "See you..."

On the way to the bathroom he thought boastfully, I could pee anywhere. In the Eiffel Tower. In a hovercraft. In Buckingham Palace, even...

Well, why not?

His aunt's loo was ordinary.

His aunt's loo was like everyone else's loo.

He took a deep breath.

"The Queen's loo, Buckingham Palace..."

Nothing to it, he thought. Just like asking for half-fare to Tottenham.

The corridor swirled.

He added hastily, "If she's not using it..."

He heard Matthew shouting, "Hey, you can't just turn up like that..."

Then there was the familiar crackle as Danny snapped through the ceilings and out into the night.

Chapter Eight

A city sparkled below him.

Was it Paris? wondered Danny.

But as he tried to pick out the Eiffel Tower, the sparkle winked out.

Darkness...

Then he saw the glitter of another city.

The glitter split into lines of street lamps as Danny skateboarded high above the river and sailed across the bright clock face of Big Ben.

London. His town.

He checked on the time. The huge metal

hands were pointing to a nine and a five. Danny looked at his watch. The pattern hadn't changed. Her time, he thought. Silly time. Didn't move. Didn't change. Had she stuck all the clocks with Super Glue?

He flew over Piccadilly Circus, skimming the dazzle of the big Coca-Cola sign and the curve of coloured stars above Regent Street. Pigeons swerved and scattered as he looped back to Trafalgar Square, swooped down past Nelson, made rings around the Christmas tree, and slid up and over the big stone arch. He could see cars moving slowly up and down The Mall. He could see the tangle of trees in St James's Park.

He skated over the head of Queen Victoria. He skated over the wrought-iron gates of the Palace. The sentries in their boxes scanned the courtyard and the street, but they didn't look up. Why should they? They were trained to deal with people on the ground, not a boy on a flying skateboard.

And snap! Danny was through the walls.

Snap! Snap! Snap! (The Palace has lots of rooms.)

Snap!
Snap!
Snap!

Snap! Snap! Snap!

He came to rest in complete darkness.

There was a faint smell of perfume. Hers? he wondered.

He stretched out his hands and found a wall. Its surface was slippery, like silk.

His fingers slid along it in search of a switch. They curled round a thing like a carved flower. They touched the middle, and the room lit up.

Danny jumped back, blinking.

Most of the light came from a chandelier. A splendid chandelier, all diamonds and rainbows. He'd seen one in a film once, but this was real, and for a second he stood there, gaping.

And above it, on the ceiling, plaster cherubs with garlands of golden flowers were dancing in a ring.

Wow! thought Danny.

This was it.

So who wanted ordinary ceilings?

And who on earth wanted silly old lamps?

Boring. Boring.

When he grew up, he was going to have gold stuff on his ceiling. And a chandelier in his bathroom.

He was going to have chandeliers all over his house...

He looked down, and suddenly saw his scuffed, laced-up boots and the turned-up ends of his jeans framed in a carpet of rich crimson. And across that carpet, two lines of gold thread made a pathway to a seat of rose-flecked marble. The seat was supported by two carved lions, and at its back lay a cushion of purple velvet, with heavy gold tassels at each corner.

And above the seat hung a canopy, with roses and thistles and shamrocks and leeks entwined round its edges, and above that, there was a statue of a lady in a long nightgown, wearing a helmet and carrying a big fork.

Danny snorted.

He thought she looked stupid.

So what? He had something important
to do.

He walked boldly up to the seat.

He hinged back the lid. The seat rim was
padded with ermine. Politely, he lifted the
rim, his fingers caressing the fur.

Across the back of the bowl the words
By Appointment were written in curly letters.
Well, he'd made one, he thought. By wishing.

He tugged at his zip.

Inside the bowl, the water was pale

turquoise and it smelt of flowers...

Danny was ready.

The turquoise greened...

When he'd finished, he reached up. In the gold handle of the chain a single ruby was glowing crimson, like that special lipstick his mum sometimes wore.

He pulled.

There should have been music or something, he thought, not that boring old *whoosh* you could have heard anywhere. A roll of drums. Trumpets, at least.

He looked down.

The water was turquoise again.

Danny felt pleased with himself. Impressed. Well, who else would have thought of peeing in the Queen's loo?

This would change everything.

He would make them all respect him now, he thought. The playground bully who called him Sambo. The skateboard show-off in Class Three who sneered, "Look at Danny the Wonderboy! Look at him wobbling!"

And his kid brother who pestered him.

And his big sister – what had she ever done? Apart from looking at her face in the mirror...

From this moment on, Danny was special.

He turned to look at the room. He wanted to remember every detail. Not that he could tell anybody. Not that anyone would believe him if he did...

He touched a roll of toilet paper held in the paws of a small jade griffin. It was gossamer-soft, and each sheet was printed with the royal coat of arms.

He carefully removed a single sheet, folded it and put it into his pocket.

On the far wall hung a marble washbasin shaped like a scallop shell and inlaid with little golden fish. When Danny filled it with water, the fish seemed to swim.

On either side of the washbasin stood two little tablets of soap – one a lion, the other a unicorn. He washed his hands with the lion, and dried them on a crimson towel initialled with the letters: E II R

How he longed to tell someone...

Suddenly he saw his reflection in the huge gilt mirror and for an instant, he was more amazed at the sight of his own familiar face – a bit sandy, a bit sweaty – than anything else.

Near the mirror, he spotted a lipstick case. He pulled off the top and wound up the stick. It was just like a crayon – a red wax crayon with a nicely sharpened point...

Chapter Nine

"Time, Danny!"

Danny whipped round guiltily. Where was she? Some of the lipstick had stuck to his fingers.

The voice came from everywhere and nowhere.

"Time, Danny!"

"Time, Danny..."

"Time, Danny..."

There was a smell of cinnamon and mothballs.

And his watch was bleeping wildly.

The skateboard came rolling across the carpet.

He stepped on to it, and the room exploded.

The chandelier sparkled and spun like a catherine wheel.

Snap! And Danny was through the wall.

Crack! Snap! And ambassadors and suits of armour, portraits and porcelain, footmen and flowers, butlers and cooks, ladies-in-waiting and corgis and kennel-maids all went flying round his head.

Crack! Snap! And he was out, skating over London, and the sky was full of giant dandelion heads of silver and fuchsia and gold.

The dandelion heads all burst into clocks.

"Puff! Twelve o'clock. Puff! One o'clock..."
Someone was telling the time. "Puff! Two
o'clock. Puff! Three. Quarter past four. Half
past four. Quarter to five and stop, stop,
stop!"

He was trying to catch some of the drifting
seeds when a black straw hat appeared
beneath him.

Danny slid into its comforting interior. Had
it grown? he wondered.

Or had she shrunk him?
He was still trying to
make up his mind as
the hat sailed down,
gentle as a shadow,
black as night, and
tipped him out on
his own doorstep.
Then it rose and
floated, like a
big balloon, up
and over the
roof-tops.

The bleep switched itself off.

Her time, thought Danny. Silly time. Crazy time.

He checked himself quickly. No, he hadn't shrunk.

He looked at his skateboard. It seemed the same, but it felt different. Heavier. Earthbound.

He put it down. The rollers rattled along the sloping path, and the curved end went crashing against the gate. Reluctantly, he went over and picked it up. She'd fixed it, he thought sadly. And now she'd unfixed it. No more flying, and he'd liked flying. And no more chandeliers; just Susie's tights dripping into the bath, and his brother's wind-up dolphin lying on its side.

And yet...

It was still his skateboard. Even without the magic. It was the nice birthday skateboard his dad had given him – maybe it was sad, too...

He swung back the gate and scootered down to the nearest lamp post. Dreamily he balanced, rocked, then, without thinking, flipped into a perfect turn.

Wow! he thought.

He tried another.

"I can do it!" he yelled. "I don't need her old magic," and to prove it, he did it again.

Cool, thought Danny.

He ran back to the house and banged at the front door.

"Come and watch!"

His sister opened it. When she saw him, she yawned.

"It's only Danny," she called out. She'd put on big, clip-on ear-rings and a silly pink bow. He thought she looked stupid.

They were all in the back room watching
television. One of the cats was asleep on the
radiator.

His mum looked up at him.

"You're late," she said. "Weren't you cold
out there?"

Danny dumped his skateboard and sat
down. Fuss, fuss, fuss. She was always
fussing. Anyone would think he was a little
kid.

And what was there to say? She wouldn't
believe him. Nobody would believe him. He
wasn't even sure he believed himself.

He put his hands in his pockets. In one of
them he found a carefully folded piece of
incredibly soft toilet paper.

He took it out and opened it.

He looked at it.

Secretly.

"Just listen to this," said his mum.

The news-reader was saying, "...A violation
of the Queen's private rooms in Buckingham
Palace is now thought to be nothing more

serious than a prank perpetrated possibly by a very junior member of the Queen's household. However, police are investigating..."

And there appeared on the screen a large mirror with a gold frame, and across its surface were crayonned the words:

Danny was here

Susie smirked, and pointed.

"Oh, yes," she said. "So that's where you've been..."

Danny put the piece of paper back into his pocket and grinned.

"As a matter of fact," he said, "it was."

He glanced out of the window into the dark night.

A small, thin shape was sailing across the stars.

It might, he supposed, have been an aeroplane...

But then, it might not.